Adapted by Alice Alfonsi

Based on the television series *Hannah Montana*, created by Michael Poryes and Rich Correll and Barry O'Brien

Part One is based on the episode written by Todd J. Greenwald

Part Two is based on the episode written by Steven Peterman and Gary Dontzig

PARRAGON

Bath · New York · Singapore · Hong Kong · Cologne · Delhi · Melbourne

First published by Parragon in 2007

Parragon
Queen Street House
4 Queen Street
Bath BA1 1HE, UK

ISBN 978-1-4075-1729-2

Printed in UK

PART ONE

Chapter One

Miley Stewart closed her eyes and fell back into Lilly Truscott's arms. She wasn't scared. Miley trusted Lilly. She knew her best friend would catch her, just as Miley had caught Lilly a few minutes before. That's what friends did for each other.

Mr. Corelli, Seaview Middle School's drama teacher, checked out the pairs around the classroom and then jumped onto the stage. "Very nice, people," he said. "Now that you have clearly mastered the trust exercise, you're ready to act."

Miley's eyes lit up. Acting was the reason she had signed up for drama class in the first place. All they had done so far were exercises.

"But," Mr. Corelli said, "the secret to acting is . . . reacting." He jumped in front of Miley's other best friend, Oliver Oken, and screamed in his face.

"Ahhhhh!" Oliver shrieked, falling back into his partner Henry's arms.

Mr. Corelli seemed pleased. "Did you see that?" he asked the class. "He reacted. He didn't think. Did you?" he asked, turning to Oliver.

"I try not to, sir," Oliver stammered, saluting.

"And you're great at it," Mr. Corelli said, saluting back.

Oliver was confused. It was the first time

anyone had ever praised him for *not* thinking.

"I want you all living in that moment," Mr. Corelli said, slowly moving in front of Miley. Suddenly he spun around. "Ahh!" he yelled, right into her face.

Miley didn't flinch. She didn't even blink. "I've got a brother," she explained. "You're going to have to do way better than that."

"Oh," Mr. Corelli said, nodding. He turned away and then spun around again. This time it was Lilly he screamed at.

Lilly jumped back and screamed, just like Oliver.

"Nice work," Mr. Corelli said. "You get an A for the day."

Lilly wasn't impressed. Mr. Corelli was definitely the strangest teacher she had ever had. "I'll take a B if you stop doing that," she said.

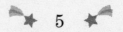

The rest of the kids in the class braced themselves. Who would Mr. Corelli pounce on next? But instead, he jumped back onstage. "Everybody, listen up! Now we're going to do the mirror exercise. What one does . . ." he raised his right hand and wiggled his fingers. "The other mirrors," he said, raising his left hand and wiggling his fingers the same way.

Miley watched him and nodded.

"Acting," Mr. Corelli said, holding his right hand in front of him like the signal for stop. "Reacting," he explained, doing the same with his left hand. Then he moved his hands together. Whatever his right hand did, his left did, too.

Miley looked at Lilly and rolled her eyes. Mr. Corelli was way too in love with his own hands.

He waved his finger in the air like a

conductor's baton. "Mirror," he commanded.

The pairs from the trust exercise stood face-to-face, mirroring each other while Mr. Corelli walked around the room, checking them out. He stopped in front of Oliver and Henry.

"Now, next week," he said. "We're doing scenes from Shakespeare's great play, *Romeo and Juliet*." He struck a dramatic pose. "But soft, what light through yonder window breaks. It is the East, and Juliet is the sun," he said, quoting Romeo.

Oliver and Henry tried to mirror him and each other, but Mr. Corelli was too caught up in his own acting to notice.

"Man, that dude knew how to pick up chicks," Mr. Corelli said, pumping his fist in the air.

Lilly and Miley tried to have a quiet

conversation while Mr. Corelli made his way around the room.

"So, who do you want for a partner?" Lilly asked.

"Well, not Oliver," Miley answered, making a face. "I mean, look at him."

Lilly turned to see Oliver scratching himself and hooting like a chimpanzee. Henry mirrored him.

Lilly snorted. "I know. He's always monkeying around." She scratched her head and her side like a monkey when she said it.

"Exactly!" Miley said, mirroring her. "And I need a good grade."

"So do I," Lilly said. "But if one of us doesn't pick him, nobody will."

Miley sighed. Lilly and Oliver were her best friends. They were the only two people in the world, except for her brother,

Jackson, and her dad, that Miley trusted with her secret.

It was a big one.

Miley Stewart led a double life. Most days she was just Miley. But at night, she became Hannah Montana. Hannah was a pop-music sensation, a queen of the teen music world. Miley loved being Hannah onstage, but offstage she was happy to take off her blond Hannah wig and pop-star clothes and go back to being Miley Stewart. She wanted people to like her for who she was, not because she was famous. That meant keeping her Hannah self under wraps. Only her best friends and her family knew the truth.

But even though Miley trusted Oliver with her secret, she didn't want to play Juliet to his Romeo. When it came to acting, Oliver was seriously bad. Miley knew

no one would pick him for a partner if one of his best friends didn't volunteer. "I guess you're right," Miley said to Lilly. "So . . ."

"You pick him," the girls said at the same time, pointing at each other. Then they pointed at themselves. "Me?" they both asked simultaneously.

Either they were expert mirrors, or Miley and Lilly both felt exactly the same way. They each put their hands on their hips at the same, exact time. "No way!" they shouted together.

"Nice mirror," Mr. Corelli said, walking by.

As soon as he was out of earshot, Lilly moved closer to Miley and lowered her voice. "I have a compromise," she said.

Miley waited. She was ready for any compromise that would let her act with anyone but Oliver.

"I pick Henry!" Lilly said, loud enough for the whole class to hear. She ran over and tapped him on the shoulder, just to prove her point.

"No fair!" Miley hissed, dragging Lilly back in front of her. "He went to Shakespeare camp three summers in a row!"

"Why do you think I picked him?" Lilly asked.

"You know what? I don't care," Miley said, her voice rising. "This doesn't mean I pick Oliver."

But all Mr. Corelli and the rest of the class heard were Miley's last three words.

"You pick Oliver?" Mr. Corelli said. "Bold choice! Especially considering you're going to have to kiss him."

Now Miley was definitely in that "moment" Mr. Corelli talked about. She didn't think. She reacted with a scream fit for a horror movie!

"I knew I'd get you!" Mr. Corelli said, laughing.

Miley didn't laugh. She clutched her cheeks. The thought of having to kiss Oliver drove the laughter out of her forever.

"Just kidding," Mr. Corelli said, knocking fists with Lilly.

Chapter Two

Miley and Oliver worked on their scene at Miley's house after school. Sometimes living on the beach at Malibu made it hard to concentrate on homework, but Miley needed to get a good grade in drama class. Of course, having to act with Oliver was going to make that hard – really hard.

Right now he was standing with his back to Miley. He had his arms wrapped around himself so it looked like someone was hugging him and running her fingers through his hair.

"Oh, Juliet," he said with an exaggerated sigh.

"Oliver," Miley snapped, spinning him around.

He cracked up, but Miley didn't appreciate the joke.

"We've been rehearsing for two hours and we're still on the first page!" she said. "It didn't take Shakespeare this long to *write* the play."

"Okay," Oliver said, holding up his hands in surrender. "Just give me a second to get into character." He turned his back on Miley and focussed on the kitchen worktop in front of him.

Why me? Miley silently howled.

"Hey, Juliet," Oliver said. Then he twirled around holding two oranges in

front of his eyes. "Get it? I'm a fruit fly? Bzzzzz." He waited for Miley to laugh.

She didn't.

"Huh? Fruit fly," he said again.

Miley swatted him with her *Romeo and Juliet* script. "Now you're a dead fruit fly," she snapped. Then she started to plead. "Can we just please do this, Oliver? Please?"

"Okay," Oliver agreed. "I'll really try this time." He struck a dramatic pose and took a deep breath. "But soft, what light over yonder breaks wind," he said, cracking up again.

"No," Miley said, shaking her head. She had had it. No way was she going to let her grades suffer because Oliver wouldn't stop fooling around. "You know what?" she asked. "I'm just going to e-mail Corelli and ask for another partner." She headed for her computer.

"Miley, wait," Oliver said, chasing after her. "I'm just nervous, okay?"

"Nervous? About what?" Miley asked.

Now Oliver got serious. "Messing up and looking stupid."

Miley didn't buy it. Talk about looking stupid, this was the same guy who spent his entire mirror time acting like a chimpanzee. "Hey, guess what," she said sarcastically. "Done that."

"At least when I joke around, they're laughing because I *want* them to," Oliver said.

"Come on, Oliver," Miley said, softening a little. "Nobody's going to laugh at you."

"Trust me," Oliver said. "This has been going on forever." He remembered that time in second grade when he had been picked to play Abraham Lincoln, his favourite president. He stood in front of the blackboard in a black suit, a black top hat and a fake Lincoln beard.

"Four score and . . ." Oliver had said nervously. He couldn't remember what came next so he started over again. "Four score and . . ." His mind was a total blank! The other second graders were starting to giggle. Oliver panicked. He pulled two oranges out of his jacket pocket and said, "I'm a fruit fly."

His classmates were still laughing, but now they were laughing at his joke, not at him. Oliver shook himself out of his memory and shared it with Miley.

Now Miley got it. Oliver had stage fright. She just had to talk him through it so that her drama grade wouldn't tank. "Okay, look, Oliver. Everybody gets nervous," she said, picking up her script again. "When I'm up there as Hannah Montana I get nervous, too."

Oliver rolled his eyes. "Oh, yeah, right," he said, not believing her. Miley always looked incredibly cool and confident in her Hannah role – even when she was singing to thousands of fans.

"No, really," Miley insisted. "The minute I hear I have to perform I get a huge knot in my stomach and my heart starts pounding so hard I can hardly move."

Just then, her father, Robby Stewart, came through the door carrying a bag of groceries. "Guess who's singing the national anthem at the Lakers game tomorrow night?" he asked with a huge smile.

Miley's face lit up. She had always wanted to sing at a Lakers game. "Yes! Hannah Montana!" she yelled, running to her father and giving him a high five. "Rocking the anthem for the Lakers!" She stopped cheering when she saw Oliver's expression.

His arms were crossed over his chest. Obviously Miley didn't look like someone with a huge knot in her stomach. Oliver knew she was totally psyched.

"But I'm nervous," she said, clutching her stomach and trying to cover her excitement. "Huge knot. I don't know if I can do it."

"Nice try," Oliver said, sarcastically.

Miley had to agree he was right. Singing in public didn't scare her – she loved being up onstage. But that didn't mean Oliver should just give in to his stage fright. "Okay, so I don't get nervous. I'm Hannah Montana, for crying out loud. I'm not a normal kid!"

Mr. Stewart saw Oliver's script on the kitchen worktop. "Wow, *Romeo and Juliet*," he said. "I had to do this scene in speech class."

"And you did just fine, didn't you?" Miley asked, nodding. If she couldn't convince Oliver that everything would be fine, maybe her father could.

"Nope," he drawled in his Tennessee accent. "Actually it was the darkest day of my life."

This wasn't helping. Miley nudged her father's arm, but he was lost in his memory. He definitely didn't read her signal.

"Made it through the first two words then froze up like Aunt Pearl in the outhouse on Christmas morning," Mr. Stewart said.

Miley kept nodding, trying to lead him to a happy ending for Oliver's – and her grade's – sake. "But everything turned out okay," she said, giving him two thumbs up.

"Only 'cause I started cracking jokes." Mr. Stewart struck a pose. "What light over yonder breaks wind," he said, quoting himself. "That one killed them."

Oliver cracked up, but Miley pinched her father's arm and glared at him.

Mr. Stewart finally got the fact that Miley was trying to send him a signal. "But that was wrong," he said seriously. "Shakespeare's very important and you'll use it every day of your life."

Miley was still glaring at him.

"Like fractions," he said. "I'm using them right now. I'm halfway out of the room, three-quarters . . ." He danced over to the stairs and then went up. "And I'm gone," he announced.

"See?" Oliver said to Miley. "I'm not the only one who had a problem with Shakespeare. Even your dad got all freaked out."

Miley had to find some way to save this situation – and her grade. "Oliver, but he didn't have me," she insisted. "You're my friend and I'm not gonna let you fall on your face."

Oliver didn't look convinced. He looked scared.

Miley snapped her fingers. She suddenly had an idea that would prove to Oliver that she wouldn't let him fail. "Here, let's do the trust exercise." She held out her arms, ready to catch her friend. "Go!" she yelled.

But just at that moment the doorbell rang. Miley turned to see who it was, and Oliver hit the floor with a thud. He sat up, rubbing his head.

"Okay, technically that wasn't your face," Miley said.

Chapter Three

The next afternoon, Miley's older brother, Jackson, was serving a customer a hot dog at Rico's Surf Shack, a beach hangout that he worked in after school. His boss's son came running up from the beach and jumped onto one of the snack bar's stools.

"Hey, Rico. How's it going?" Jackson asked.

"Great, fine, swell," Rico said anxiously.

 23

"Now give me my box. Where's my secret candy box?"

Jackson handed Rico a biscuit tin.

Rico grabbed it and then looked inside. It was empty! "Ahhhhhh!" Rico screamed. "Where is it? What happened?" He grabbed Jackson by the T-shirt and pulled him closer. "What did you do? It's gone!" he said between clenched teeth.

"Yeah, along with the enamel on your teeth," Jackson said, pulling Rico's hand off his shirt. "Look, your dad called. Your last dental exam was so bad, they're putting your X-rays up in the lobby to scare the other kids."

"The man lies!" Rico yelled. He was desperate for his afternoon sugar rush. He'd say anything to get his sweets. "Last time we went to the movies, he put me in a diaper so I'd get in for free."

Jackson shook his head. "No, I'm not buying it," he said. He remembered the time Rico paid a beauty school student to shave Jackson's head, and the time he lost a bet and Rico forced Jackson to dress up like a girl and assist him in his magic act. Rico's dad had given Jackson the perfect opportunity for payback. "This is the same father who gave me a hundred bucks to keep this away from you?" Jackson waved a plastic bag full of sweets in Rico's face.

"Gimme, gimme, gimme." Rico reached for the sweets, pleading, but Jackson held the bag just out of his reach.

"Settle down, all right?" Jackson said. "See what these sweets are doing to you? This is for your own good." He didn't add that if it made Rico miserable, it was also great entertainment for Jackson.

"Fine," Rico snapped. "But listen to me

and listen good. There's not a place on this earth where you could put that candy that I'm not gonna get it."

"Oh, yeah," Jackson teased. "What about right here?" He popped a sweet into his mouth.

That set Rico off again. "Gimme, gimme, gimme," he begged.

But Jackson was having too much fun. "And here," he said, eating another one. "And here."

Rico jumped onto the counter and then over it, right on top of Jackson. Customers peered over the counter, their mouths open in shock, while Jackson and Rico wrestled for the sweets.

A couple of hours later, Jackson dashed in the back door of the Stewart house. He had finished off Rico's entire stash of sweets and bought a few chocolate bars on the way home.

Mr. Stewart was making dinner.

"Hey, Dad, how you doing?" Jackson babbled. "What's for dinner? Hope it's meat loaf. How was your day? Mine was good. Nice shirt. Goes with your hair. What's for dinner? Did I already ask that? Meat loaf?" He tried to slow his words down, but they all came out in one big rush – one big *sugar* rush.

Mr. Stewart had seen this before. "Jackson, how much candy have you had today?" he asked.

Jackson's eyes popped. "Wh- wh- wh-why would you even ask that?"

"We both know you have a problem when you've had too many sweets," his father answered.

"Let it go. I was eight. It was Easter. I'd

never seen a chocolate bunny before," Jackson said. He talked so fast that he could hardly get the words out, but then the idea of a chocolate bunny slowed him down. "Mmm," he said, as if he were in a trance, "big chocolate bunny ears with candy eyes . . ."

Mr. Stewart had heard enough. "Okay, let me smell your breath," he said.

Jackson knew his candy breath would give him away. He pressed his lips together and blew a little air in his father's direction.

But even that little bit was enough to confirm Mr. Stewart's suspicions. "Dang, you smell like the inside of a piñata."

Jackson shrugged. "Big deal. So I had a few dozen pieces of candy. I can stop anytime I want." He headed upstairs, pulling a chocolate bar out of his pocket and smelling the rich chocolatey smell through the wrapper.

Miley passed him on her way down for dinner. "Hey, what're you eating?" she asked.

Jackson panicked. Was she after his chocolate? "Nothing!" he shouted. "Get off my back, woman!"

Uh-oh, Miley thought. Jackson's gone overboard with the sugar again. She watched him run upstairs clutching his chocolate and then sat at the kitchen worktop. "Daddy, I haven't seen him like this since Halloween of '99."

"Oh, I remember," Mr. Stewart said, shaking his head. "I clocked him at fifty-eight miles an hour on his roller skates in a Yoda costume." He added pepper and barbecue sauce to his meat loaf mixture and then he changed the subject. "So, how's it going with Romeo?"

"Well, I finally got Oliver to take it

seriously and guess what?" Miley asked. "He's seriously HORRIBLE!"

"I think you guys need to take a break," her father said. "We'll go to the Lakers game, you'll sing the anthem, get your mind off it."

Miley rolled her eyes. "I wish," she said with a sigh. "But all I can think about is getting a bad grade and looking stupid just because I got stuck with Oliver."

Mr. Stewart's eyes met Oliver's, who had come in just in time to hear Miley's last sentence. "Mile, Oliver is –"

"I know," Miley said, cutting him off. "He's a friend and you don't bail out on friends."

Her father tried again. "Yeah, Mile, but –"

"But nothing," Miley said, getting more worked up. "It's like he's the *Titanic* and

I've got to jump ship before I go down with him."

Oliver gaped at the back of her head. He couldn't believe that one of his best friends was actually saying those things about him. Especially after she promised to help him.

"Uh, iceberg right behind you," Mr. Stewart said, finally getting Miley's attention.

She whirled around to see Oliver glaring at her.

"You said you'd be there for me," he said sadly.

Miley tried to explain. "Oliver, I was just —"

But Oliver had heard all he needed to hear. "Bailing out on me," he said.

"No, I was just *thinking* about bailing out on you – it's different," Miley said, trying to save the situation.

"You said I was the *Titanic*," Oliver said over his shoulder, just before he stormed out of the house.

"Not the ship," Miley called after him. "The very successful movie! You made, like, a billion dollars." But it was too late. Oliver was gone. She turned to her dad. "Okay, Daddy, we need a new warning signal."

"Honey, I did everything but baste you with barbecue sauce," he said.

"I should not feel bad about this!" Miley said, trying to push away her guilty feelings. "It's not my fault Shakespeare makes him nervous. 'What light through yonder window breaks?' How tough is that?"

A few hours later, Miley had transformed herself into Hannah. She wore a long blond wig and cool pop-star clothes, and she flashed a big grin while she listened to the announcer introduce her to the crowd: "Ladies and gentlemen, please rise for the singing of our national anthem by teen pop sensation Hannah Montana!"

Miley stepped into the spotlight, smiled at the cheering crowd and started to sing in the strong voice that had made her famous. "Oh, say, can you see, by the dawn's early light. Through yonder window breaks."

Her eyes darted around nervously. She had mixed Shakespeare's dialogue into the words of the song! She had just flubbed the words to "The Star-Spangled Banner"!

"Uhhhh," she said, trying to remember what came next. "Rampart's . . . no, rockets red glare. Yeah, right," she said. "That's right." But what came next? She couldn't remember.

"You stink!" she heard somebody yell.

The Lakers fans laughed and booed. Hannah had never been booed before. Miley didn't know what to do, except duck when the crowd starting pelting her with buckets of popcorn, hot dog rolls and cups full of fizzy drink.

In desperation, she did the only thing she could think of. She grabbed two empty cups and put them over her eyes. "Look! I'm a cup fly," she said. "Ya get it? Buzz."

But the crowd didn't get it. They were too busy booing.

Chapter Four

The next day, Mr. Stewart flipped pancakes while Jackson sat at the kitchen table squeezing maple syrup onto his plate.

"Jackson, you want some pancakes with that syrup?" Mr. Stewart asked.

"No, thanks. I'm good." Jackson pulled a curly straw out of his pocket and started slurping. Who needed pancakes?

"Jumping Jehoshaphat, son!" Mr. Stewart said, with a look of disgust on his face. "Next time, don't waste a plate. Just drink it from the bottle."

Jackson didn't hear the sarcasm in his father's voice. He was too intent on getting his sugar fix. "Oh, that's a great idea!" He put his straw directly in the syrup bottle and took a big sip. "Whoa!" he said, feeling the sugar rushing through his body. "That really worked. Thanks, Dad."

Mr. Stewart shook his head while Jackson rushed out of the back door, syrup bottle in hand. He passed Lilly on his way out.

"Sweet," Lilly said, nodding and smiling when she saw the syrup bottle.

"It's good!" Jackson said, just before he ran off.

"Hey, Mr. Stewart," Lilly said. "How's Miley?"

Mr. Stewart cleared Jackson's syrup

plate off the table. "Well, it's noon and she's still holed up in her room, if that tells you anything."

Just then, Miley trudged down the stairs. She was still wearing her pyjamas and carried a fuzzy teddy bear.

"Hey, bud," her dad said. "How you doing?"

"Okay," she said. "Except I had this awful dream where I forgot the national anthem in front of thousands of people."

Uh-oh, Lilly thought. Her best friend had not only forgotten the words to the anthem, she forgot she forgot! "Uh, that wasn't a dream," Lilly said.

Miley rolled her eyes. She knew it was real, but she wanted to block the whole thing out of her mind. "You couldn't play along for, like, a minute?" she asked.

"Oh, sorry," Lilly said. "Let's not talk

about it anymore. Let's watch some TV. Get your mind off it." She steered Miley to the sofa and grabbed the remote.

Miley's own face filled the TV screen. She was just at the point of the song where she totally messed up. "Everyone is talking about Hannah Montana's massive mistake," said the newscaster.

Miley held her bear's ears so he wouldn't have to listen.

Lilly changed the channel, only to find Hannah Montana on-screen again, doing her imitation of a cup fly. This announcement was in Spanish, but Miley could still understand it. "Ha, ha, ha!" meant the same thing in any language.

Okay, so watching TV turned out to be a colossally bad idea, Lilly thought. She turned it off.

Miley turned the bear around so they

were nose to nose. "I am so sorry you had to see that, Bearie," she said, kissing his nose.

"Bearie the bear?" Lilly asked, raising her eyebrows. "You couldn't do any better than that?"

"I was three!" Miley said. "And I'm not changing his name now. That would just confuse him."

She jumped to her feet and walked towards the kitchen.

"Here you go, Mile," her father said, putting a plate of pancakes down on the worktop. They were Miley's favourite.

"I'm too upset to eat," Miley said, slumping onto a stool.

"I'm not." Lilly sat down and pulled the plate in front of her.

The pancakes hadn't improved Miley's mood, but Mr. Stewart had something else he was sure would cheer her up. "Well, listen. After tonight, when Hannah performs on *Top Rockers*, nobody's even going to remember she screwed up the national anthem."

"What?" Miley yelled.

"*Top Rockers*? I love that show!" Lilly said.

"Made the call this morning," Mr. Stewart said. "It's all set."

Miley didn't share Lilly's excitement. "Daddy, I can't perform on *Top Rockers*. That's a live show. What if I mess up again?"

"Miley, what's going on?" Lilly asked. "You've never had stage fright before." She swallowed a bite of her pancakes and turned to Mr. Stewart. "These are very good. What did you do to them?"

Mr. Stewart nodded his thanks, but

Miley had other things on her mind. Like last night's disaster.

"I mean, I never had people laughing at me before," she said.

"Mile, that's not gonna happen again," her father said and then he turned to Lilly. "Actually, I just put in a splash of vanilla and a hint of cinnamon."

Miley couldn't believe they were talking about pancakes when she was in danger of being laughed at by thousands of people for the second day in a row. "Daddy!" she moaned.

"Mile, listen," her father said. "If you want to put this thing behind you, you've got to get back on the horse. Just like Uncle Earl."

Miley's forehead wrinkled in confusion. "Uncle Earl forgot the words to the national anthem?"

"No, Uncle Earl fell off a horse," her father explained. "It took four of us to get that fat old coot back up."

"I just don't want to get laughed at again," Miley said sadly.

"Wow," Lilly said innocently. "That's exactly how Oliver feels and you bailed out on him. Ironic, isn't it?"

But Miley didn't want to believe that what had happened to her the previous night was anything like what Oliver was afraid of. And she didn't want to be reminded of the fact that Oliver wasn't speaking to her. "Stop your flapping and eat your flapjacks," she said sarcastically.

"Mile, everybody gets nervous," her father said. "But the longer you wait, the tougher it's going to get."

Miley thought about that for a second. Sooner or later, Hannah Montana was going to have to face the world again. It might as well be tonight on *Top Rockers*. "I guess you're right," she said. "I've just got to do this, haven't I?" But then all kinds of disaster scenarios started to rush through her mind. "But what if I forget the words to one of my songs? Or I forget to put my costume on?" Miley gasped. "Then I'd be singing in my underwear!"

"That'd be quite a show," Lilly said, not taking Miley's concerns seriously.

But Miley's response to her best friend was cut off when Jackson burst through the front door and slammed it behind him. A crowd of angry bees crashed into the glass, buzzing like crazy. Jackson had finished off his syrup bottle and stolen a beehive.

"Stupid, selfish bees," Jackson yelled at them, then slurped the honey off his hand. "How much honey do you need?"

* * *

That afternoon, Lilly followed Oliver as he left the beach.

"Come on, Oliver," she urged. "Miley really needs us there tonight. You can't just bail out on her."

"Oh, you mean like she did to me?" he asked.

"But she knows how you feel now," Lilly said, jumping in front of him to stop him from leaving. "Leonardo DiCaprio threw a foam finger at her. Hasn't she suffered enough?"

"Let me think." Oliver pretended to take a moment. "No," he said firmly, pushing past her.

But Lilly wasn't ready to give up – she ran after him, calling his name.

Chapter Five

Two chocolate bunnies sat on top of the counter at Rico's. It looked like they were getting ready for a bunny puppet show.

Jackson crouched behind the counter. "Oh, here we are in Happy Bunnyland, Tokyo," he said in a high-pitched voice.

There was a loud pounding from underneath the counter.

"Oh, no, what's that?" Jackson asked in his bunny voice. Then he answered his own question. "It's Jack-zilla! Run for your lives!"

Jackson's head peeked out from behind the counter. He gave the bunnies his meanest Jack-zilla glare and flicked his tongue like a giant lizard before grabbing the bunnies with a roar. He tore off one set of ears with a big chomp of his Jack-zilla teeth.

He was working his way down to the bunny's feet when he felt someone's eyes staring at him – mockingly. Rico sat at the counter, chewing a carrot.

"What are you looking at?" Jackson asked defensively.

"Jackson, you have to stop," Rico said. "You're hopping down a bunny trail of no return." He reached out to take the chocolate away.

Jackson snatched it back. "You don't know what you're talking about," he said.

"Of course I do," Rico answered calmly. "I was like you once. But I'm a veggie man now." He jumped off his stool and started shadow boxing. "I even worked out this morning. It's like I have the energy of a five-year-old again."

Jackson rolled his eyes. Big deal. He had energy, too – sugar-rush energy. So what if it left him feeling tired and draggy when it wore off? That problem was easily solved by more sweets. "Great. Tell it to someone who cares."

"When you're ready to get that candy monkey off your back," Rico said seriously, "call me." He held out a card.

Jackson grabbed it from him and watched Rico run to the beach, full of healthy energy. "Well, I don't need help, all right?" he yelled after him. "I'm perfectly fine." I am perfectly fine, he told himself again, taking another bite of his bunny. He watched a little girl and her mother walk past the snack bar. The little girl dropped her ice-cream cone in the sand.

"Oh, dear. Don't pick that up, honey," her mother said. "We'll get another."

The girl and her mother walked back towards the ice-cream parlour, but Jackson couldn't take his eyes off the cone in the sand. He stared at it, licking his lips. The ice-cream was calling to him. It didn't want to melt there in the sand. It wanted to be in his belly. Jackson had to save that ice-cream cone!

He leaped over the counter and ran to it. Crouching down in the sand, Jackson took a big bite. He ignored the sand – what harm could a little sand do? – as he gobbled it down. Suddenly, he realized what he was doing, but somehow he couldn't stop.

"What's happening to me?" he cried, taking another big bite.

After work, Jackson hung out on a beach chair with his chocolate bars and watched the surfers. Then he started to doze off.

Rico walked up with a pretty girl on each arm. He was covered in muscles. "Hey, Jackson," he said. "Beautiful day for a walk, isn't it?"

Jackson was covered in sweet wrappers and he was huge. He felt as if he had gained 300 pounds in minutes. "And some pretty ladies to go for a walk with," Jackson said. "Hey, guys, wait up. I'll walk with you."

But they didn't hear him and Jackson was so big he couldn't get out of the chair. He grunted as he tried to wriggle himself out from between the arms of the chair.

"See, girls?" Rico said, looking over his

shoulder. "That's what too much sugar will do."

The girls giggled and the three of them walked off while Jackson tried to heave himself out of the chair. Finally he was out. "C'mon, guys, wait up," he said. "You're a speedy little guy, aren't you? C'mon, guys."

Jackson tried running to catch up with them, but his arms and legs were so fat that he could hardly move and he fell down on his back. He waved his arms and legs in the air. He couldn't stand up. "Help me," he called. "Help me." But Rico and the girls were already halfway down the beach.

"Help me," Jackson called again. He woke up with a start. It was a dream, he realized with relief. Just a dream. Except he was covered in sweet wrappers, just like in the dream, and he had a half-eaten chocolate bar clutched in one hand.

He patted his arms and legs. They were normal size. "I can see my feet again," he realized. "My skinny, skinny little feet." He eyed the chocolate in his hand and made a resolution. "That's it," he said to it. "That is it! You don't own me anymore, old devil sugar."

Jackson jumped to his feet and threw the chocolate in the nearest rubbish bin. He started to run away. Was the chocolate calling to him? Could he really give it up? Jackson reached his arms out to the rubbish bin. "I love you," he mouthed silently. Then he did it. He turned his back on the chocolate, left the beach and ran home.

Miley, wearing her Hannah Montana clothes and long blond wig, sat backstage at *Top Rockers* nervously jiggling her legs. She tried to remember the words to her first song, but the memory of last night's boos and laughter at the Lakers game was looping around in her brain. What if it happened again?

Mr. Stewart, wearing the dark wig and moustache disguise that transformed him from Miley's dad to Hannah's manager, tried to reassure her. "Now, bud, you've done this a million times. You've got nothing to be nervous about."

"Then why am I sweating through my wig?" Miley asked.

"You're going to do fine," her father said, patting her head. "I've got all the confidence in the world in you." He wiped his hand on his shirt and headed in the direction of the stage manager. "Okay, just remember," he whispered. "If her mouth is open and nothing's coming out, you cut to a commercial."

The stage manager nodded.

Mr. Stewart turned back to Miley and gave her a thumbs-up. "No worries, honey."

Miley gave him a thumbs-up in return, but the look on her face didn't exactly inspire confidence.

Mr. Stewart realized that this could turn out to be another disaster. He leaned towards the stage manager. "And I mean it," he whispered. A commercial was better than the sight of Hannah Montana opening and closing her mouth with nothing coming out. He headed off to make sure all the stagehands knew what to do.

Lilly came backstage carrying a bunch of Hannah Montana posters. She wore the disguise she always wore when she hung out with Hannah – a purple wig, lots of make-up and wilder clothes than she normally wore. It was all part of Miley's plan to keep her Hannah Montana life a secret from everyone who knew her as Miley.

"Lola!" Miley said, using the name Lilly picked for her disguise. "I can't remember anything. What am I going to do?"

"Don't worry," Lilly said. "I've got it sorted." She held up several Hannah Montana posters to show Miley that she had written the lyrics to her songs on the backs of them.

"Oh, cue cards. Great idea," Miley said, sounding a little relieved. Then she went back into panic mode. "What if I forget how to read?"

"Get a grip," Lilly said. "This is the life, hold on tight. This is the dream, it's all you need."

"Hey, you're right," Miley said. "That's great advice."

Lilly's eyes popped. Things were worse than she thought. "What advice? Those are the lyrics to your song!"

"Of course they are," Miley said. "I'm not nervous. I'm good."

"Places, Miss Montana," the stage manager said.

Miley grabbed Lilly's arms. "Help me!" she pleaded.

"I will," Lilly said, trying to calm her friend down. "Just remember, keep your eyes on me."

"Right," Miley nodded. "What song is that from?"

"That's not a song. That was the advice!" Lilly said. "Oh, boy." She let out a sigh. She wondered if Miley was going to be able to get past this.

They peeked out at the audience just in time to see Oliver taking a seat.

"Oh, great," Miley said. "What's Oliver doing here?"

"Maybe he came to support a friend," Lilly said.

"Or maybe he came to laugh at me," Miley said. He was still pretty mad at her about the whole Shakespeare thing.

Lilly didn't want to get into another whole discussion about Oliver. There wasn't time. "Could be," she said. "Either way, good luck."

Chapter Six

Miley stood in the wings while Lilly made her way into the audience with her cue cards. This was it, Miley thought. *Top Rockers* was an acoustic show, so she wouldn't be surrounded by her band and backup dancers. It was just Miley and her audience. A single guitar player sat at the back of the stage.

The stage manager began the countdown. "Four . . . three . . . two . . ."

The lights slowly came up and Miley listened to the announcer introduce her: "And now, live and acoustic, *Top Rockers* is proud to present, Hannah Montana!"

The crowd cheered and clapped and Miley took the stage, smiling and waving. She calmed down a little, remembering how much her fans loved her. Then the doubt came back. What if she forgot her lyrics? Thank goodness Lilly was out there with those cue cards.

Miley grabbed the microphone and started singing her most popular song. She nodded at Lilly and watched her turn a "Hannah Rocks" poster around so Miley could see the lyrics. This is *perfect*, thought Miley. Even if I forget the words, it's okay because they're right in front of me!

When Lilly switched to her second cue card, she started swaying to the beat of the music. Miley had to sway back and forth, too, to be able to read the words. At first, it was fine, but then Lilly really started getting into it. She was bopping to the music and got so caught up in the song that she forgot to switch to the next cue card!

Miley tried to signal to Lilly with her eyes, then with her tone of voice. She didn't know what to do. In her panic over the cue cards, she'd forgotten the next line! Well, she had no choice. She'd just sing the same line over and over . . . and over.

Finally Lilly got the point and switched the card, but the guy behind her was tired of looking at Hannah Montana signs instead of Hannah herself. "Down in front," he yelled.

Lilly squatted and moved to the side, but now her cue card was directly behind a guy with an enormous head of hair.

Miley couldn't see the sign. And she couldn't remember the words. "Dah, dah, dah life," she stammered. "Hold on tight."

Lilly moved around with the cards, but wherever she ended up, Miley's view was blocked. Miley cringed, trying to remember the words. All she could sing was nonsense.

"Dah, dah, dah. It's all I la. Na-na-na-na," Miley sang nervously.

Finally Lilly came to an open spot, but now her cue card was upside down! Miley had to do a back bend and try to read and sing at the same time. "You'll never know where you'll dah. And I'm gonna take my . . . shabbah dah."

Lilly tried to turn her cue cards rightside up. But she banged into someone and fell right off the row of seats. The cue cards went flying.

"I'm still getting it . . . wrong," Miley sang, slumping to the stage.

The guitarist played a few more chords, confused about what to do next. But Miley had given up. Her career was over. She couldn't remember her lyrics. Everyone would laugh at her now.

Oliver jumped to his feet. "Hold on tight," he sang, his voice quavering. He signalled to the audience to join in and the guitarist started to play again.

Relief flooded through Miley. Suddenly she was herself again. Her stage fright was gone. She got to her feet with a huge smile and started singing, her voice stronger than ever.

She waved and winked at Oliver to let him know how much his support meant to her. He smiled back. They were friends again.

Mr. Stewart nudged the stage manager. "And you were worried," he teased.

Lilly got to her feet just in time to join the crowd as they cheered for Miley. Hannah Montana was back! She was able to finish the song herself – no cue cards needed.

An hour later, when Miley came to the last verse of her last song, there was no question that she was back. Her voice filled the room and she was full of confidence again.

The crowd cheered.

"Thank you, all," Miley said when the song had ended. Then she got serious. "You know I had a rough patch at the beginning of the show and an even rougher patch earlier this week. But I learned something I should've known all along." She stared

"We've been rehearsing for two hours and we're still on the first page!" Miley said. "It didn't take Shakespeare this long to *write* the play."

"Okay, I'll really try this time," Oliver said. He struck a dramatic pose. "But soft, what light over yonder breaks wind," he said, cracking up.

"I'm just nervous, okay?" Oliver said.
"About what?" Miley asked.
Now Oliver got serious. "Messing up and looking stupid."

"Guess who's singing the national anthem at the Lakers
game tomorrow night?" Mr Stewart asked as he
came through the door.

But when Miley stepped into the spotlight to sing the national anthem as Hannah Montana, she suddenly forgot the words! Miley wondered if Oliver's nervousness was contagious.

"I had this awful dream where I forgot the national anthem in front of thousands of people," Miley said. "Uh, that wasn't a dream," Lilly said.

"I learned something I should've known all along," Hannah said, staring directly at Oliver and Lilly. "Good friends don't bail out on you. And they're always there to catch you if you fall."

"I don't think I can do this," Oliver whispered to Miley. "Yes, you can," Miley said. "You were there for me and I'm going to be there for you."

"These days, my life's all about managing Hannah
Montana – and that's just the way I like it,"
said Mr Stewart, who had once been known as Robby
Ray, the Honky-tonk Heartthrob.

As Hannah and Mr Stewart were about to leave the Tipton
Hotel and head to the airport, Maddie said,
"I couldn't live with myself if I knew I was the person holding
Robby Ray back from howlin' again."

Lilly came over when Miley got back to Malibu.
"You should have seen the look on his face when
that girl in Boston recognized him.
I know he misses being onstage."

Everyone gathered to watch an old tape of Mr Stewart
performing as Robby Ray. "You were incredible.
Why aren't you still performing?" Lilly asked.

"If you want to go out and 'howl with the dogs,'
there's nothing holding you back," said Miley.

"Sweetheart, that was ten years ago,"
Mr Stewart said. "I bet my old manager
doesn't even remember my name."

"Mile, why are you pushing so hard?" asked Mr Stewart. "Because of the way I feel when I'm onstage," Miley replied. "Don't you remember that feeling?"

After the show, Miley and Jackson went backstage. "You were great," said Jackson.

directly at Oliver and Lilly. "Good friends don't bail out on you. And they're always there to catch you if you fall."

"We love you Hannah!" Lilly and Oliver shouted together.

"I love you, too!" Miley shouted back. "I love you all. Thank you everybody. Good night!"

The next day in class, Miley and Oliver had dressed up in Elizabethan costumes for their drama class scene. The costumes were Miley's inspiration. She always felt more like Hannah when she put on the blond wig and her Hannah clothes. She thought the costumes might help Oliver feel more like Romeo.

Most of the class had already done their scenes. Lilly and Henry were onstage, doing an amazing job.

"I don't think I can do this," Oliver whispered to Miley.

"C'mon, Oliver," Miley said. "You've just got to stay positive."

"Okay. I'm positive I can't do this."

"Yes, you can," Miley said. "You were there for me and I'm going to be there for you."

Lilly and Henry finished their scene. The class applauded.

"Ah! I love the energy I've seen today," Mr. Corelli said. "I love the passion. But most of all, I love that we're almost done." He turned to Miley and Oliver. "Stewart, Oken, take us home, please."

Oliver gulped as they took their places on the stage. They had to do the final scene – the death scene.

"Okay, remember," Miley whispered. "All you have to do is die."

Oliver nodded. He laid down on the stage. Miley sat, leaning over him with a look of pure grief on her face.

"Oh, Romeo," she said dramatically. "Poison, I see, hath been his timeless end. Oh, Romeo."

Oliver lifted his head slightly. "And now I die," he gasped, falling back again.

It was time for Miley's last lines, but Oliver suddenly sat up with a death rattle. He clutched his throat and pretended to be struggling for breath.

Miley stared at him with her mouth open. What was he doing?

The class tried not to laugh while Oliver twitched and moaned and gasped.

The bell rang. Mr. Corelli and the rest of the class filed out while Oliver kept dying and dying and dying. "I see the light," he gasped.

"Again, longer than it took him to write the play!" Miley yelled, cutting him off. But then she smiled. Oliver was definitely over his stage fright. And he may have been a ham, but at least he wasn't a fruit fly.

PART TWO

Chapter One

Miley shoved one last thing into her suitcase and tried to close it. Why was it that she always ended a Hannah Montana tour with so much more stuff than she started out with? All she did was buy some souvenirs – a cool new outfit or two in a Boston boutique, presents for Lilly, Oliver and Jackson – and accept a few gifts from fans. It was a good thing she was travelling as Hannah Montana and not as Miley Stewart, because there was no way her Hannah wig was going to fit in that suitcase.

Miley pressed down on the top of the suitcase. The two halves of the zip were still a couple of inches apart. Then she sat on it, but that didn't work, either.

"Darlin', have you finished packing yet?" Mr. Stewart called from his adjoining room in Boston's Tipton Hotel. "We've got to get to the airport."

"Almost done it," Miley said. "Ah, Daddy, got any room in your suitcase?" She plopped her butt on the suitcase again and slid right off it and onto the floor with a *thump*.

Mr. Stewart came into Miley's room wearing his Robby Ray disguise – it was the look he wore when he was acting as Hannah Montana's manager, not Miley Stewart's dad.

Miley tried to close her suitcase again. "Dad, you got any room in your su –"

"No," Mr. Stewart said, cutting her off. Half of his suitcase was already filled with things Miley "had to have" and couldn't fit into her own bags.

"But, you've got that zip –"

"No," Mr. Stewart said again.

But Miley wasn't ready to give up. Every single thing in her suitcase was valuable. She couldn't leave one thing behind. "And what about that carry-on case?"

"No." Mr. Stewart headed back to his own room before she could work on him some more. Soon he'd be travelling with just the clothes on his back and a suitcase full of Miley's things.

Hannah Montana's bodyguard, Roxy, opened the door. Maddie, one of the new friends Miley had made on the Boston leg of her Hannah Montana tour, was waiting to say goodbye.

"Excuse me, Miss Montana," Roxy said, blocking the doorway. "There's a girl out here who wants to see you. Claims she's Maddie from the candy counter. You want me to tell her you're not here?"

Roxy took her bodyguard duties seriously. Most of the time, Miley was happy knowing that Roxy was watching her back. Roxy would do anything to protect her. But every once in a while, Roxy used her Marine training to scare fans – and friends.

Not here? Maddie's eyes darted from Roxy to Hannah and back to Roxy again. "But she's right there," Maddie said, pointing. "I can see her."

"Not if her bodyguard says you can't," Roxy declared.

"Sorry, Hannah, can't see you," Maddie yelled over Roxy's shoulder. "By the way, love the top!"

"Hey, Roxy," Miley said, smiling. "She's a friend of mine. She can come in."

Roxy didn't take her eyes off Maddie. "You're in luck," she said seriously. "She's here." The bodyguard stepped aside and watched Maddie bounce into the room before closing the door. Then she immediately opened it again. She pointed at her own eyes with two fingers and then turned them on Maddie before pointing at herself again. "I've got my eyes on you," she warned.

Miley shook her head with a smile. Roxy could be too much sometimes, but right now the real problem was getting her suitcase closed. "Hey, Maddie," she said. "Just the tush I've been looking for. Can you close my suitcase?"

"Wait till I tell my friends that I sat on Hannah Montana's suitcase!" Maddie said, happily jumping on top of it. But the case still didn't close.

"You're not heavy enough," Miley said with a frown. Then she spotted a couple of phone books on the side table. "Here, hold these phone books." Miley piled the thick phone books in Maddie's outstretched arms.

"I just wanted to say goodbye and thank you for the tickets. Your concert was awesome," Maddie said.

"Thanks," Miley answered, but her mind was elsewhere. "Now bounce up and down."

"Well, we are a full-service hotel," Maddie joked.

Miley struggled to zip up the case while Maddie bounced, but it wasn't working.

The girls heard Mr. Stewart singing in the next room.

"I want my mullet back," he crooned in his Tennessee drawl. "My old Camaro and my eight-track."

Maddie stopped bouncing and stood up, putting the phone books back on the table. "Wow, that guy sounds just like the singer my mum used to listen to." She shook her head, trying to remember his name. "Wow, what did they call him? You know, the Honky-tonk Heartthrob . . ."

Miley was too busy trying to close her suitcase to pay too much attention. "Oh, you're talking about Robby Ray?" It wasn't just the name her dad used as Hannah's Montana's manager. It was also his old stage name. Maddie, of course, didn't know Miley's secret. She knew Hannah Montana, but she didn't know that

Hannah was really Miley Stewart.

"Yeah, yeah," Maddie said, her voice rising with excitement. "That's the guy. He had a couple of top-ten songs."

Mr. Stewart couldn't resist. "Actually three number ones, two top fives," he said, walking in from the next room. "Music video of the year. But who's counting?"

Maddie started jumping up and down when she got a look at him. "Oh, my gosh, you're Robby Ray! My mum thought you were dead! She's going to be so excited you're alive!"

"I'm kind of happy about that myself," Mr. Stewart teased.

Miley wasn't ready to join the Robby Ray fan club. She had a problem to solve. "Yeah, what about if we take some of the happy and put some of that here?" she said, pointing to her suitcase.

"I'm on the case." Mr. Stewart plopped down on the suitcase and Miley was finally able to get the zip closed.

"So, why aren't you still performing?" Maddie asked.

"Oh, no, this ol' dog stopped howlin' a long time ago," Mr. Stewart said, shaking his head.

"Howlin' Dogs!" Maddie squealed. "That was my mum's favourite album. Don't you miss singing?"

Mr. Stewart shrugged. "Oh, maybe a little."

"Wow," Maddie said, amazed. "It must have taken something huge to make you walk away from a career like that."

Mr. Stewart looked at Miley with a smile. "Yeah, it did." He put his arm around his daughter. "These days, my life's all about managing Hannah Montana – and that's just the way I like it." He turned to Miley. "Well, darlin', we have a plane to catch. Let's get ready to head to the airport."

"Man, I couldn't live with myself if I knew I was the person holding Robby Ray back from howlin' again," Maddie said, watching Mr. Stewart walk into his own room to grab his suitcase.

Holding Robby Ray back from howling? Miley felt like Maddie had just dropped a big bomb in the middle of the room. She knew her dad had given up his singing career, but she never thought about the reasons why. Was Maddie right? Did she hold her dad back? Would he be happier performing than parenting?

Maddie was totally unaware of the effect of her words. "Wow, well, it was nice meeting you," she said brightly. "I hope you enjoyed your stay at the Tipton Hotel."

"Holding him back?" Miley said to herself, watching Maddie leave. Then she made a decision. "Well, not for long," she announced to the walls before pulling her suitcase off the bed. The weight of it sent her crashing to the floor.

Chapter Two

Back home in Malibu the next day, Miley and Lilly went through a box of old Robby Ray souvenirs.

"I can't believe that this is your dad," Lilly said, holding up an old record album. Robby Ray's hair took up most of the front cover. "It's lucky records were so big. There's no way you'd fit all that hair on a CD," Lilly joked.

Miley found an old concert T-shirt. A

young Robby Ray looked out at her from the front. "It's called a mullet," she said, trying to explain the weird hairstyle. Her dad's hair was short in front but long in back. The T-shirt said it all. "'Business in the front,'" she read and then she turned the T-shirt around. The back of Robby Ray's head, with long hair, was on the flip side. "A 'party in the back,'" she read. "Oh, yeah!"

Lilly couldn't believe it. "Before your dad was a dad, he was cool. Before my dad was a dad, he was an accountant," she said, trying to sound enthusiastic. "Addition in the front, subtraction in the back!"

Miley gazed blankly at her. What could she say, hooray for maths?

"It's not the same thing, is it?" Lilly asked, a little embarrassed.

Miley shook her head, but really she was

already thinking about something else. "You should've seen the look on his face when that girl in Boston recognized him. I don't care what he says. I know he misses being onstage."

"Whoa!" Lilly said, looking into the box. "He even had his own doll!"

Miley pulled a mullet-haired doll out of the box and pulled the string in its back. "Eee, doggies," the Robby Ray doll said.

Jackson carried another box downstairs. A videotape rested on top. "You guys have got to check this out. It's labelled Robby Palooza." He put the tape in the VCR and turned on the TV.

Miley sat next to Jackson on the sofa. "Cool! Dad had his own Palooza."

Lilly was still trying to find something equally cool about her own dad. "My dad had his own calculator," she said.

Miley and Jackson rolled their eyes and focussed on the TV. Robby Ray was singing to thousands of screaming fans.

"Look how much fun he's having," Miley said.

"I can't believe it." Lilly turned to her best friend. "You've got a great voice and he's awesome," she said, pointing to Robby Ray on the TV. Then she focussed on Jackson. "What's your talent?"

"Oh, well, I don't like to brag, but . . ." Jackson stood and did some armpit farts. "And when I'm clammy, I can do it behind the knees," he said proudly.

He was still doing armpit farts when Mr. Stewart walked into the room. "Slow down, son," he warned. "You're gonna give yourself another rash." Then he noticed the TV. "Whoa, Robby Palooza! What are you watching this old thing for?"

"Mr. Stewart, you were incredible," Lilly said. "What happened?"

Mr. Stewart simply looked at her. Wasn't he incredible still?

"I mean, why aren't you still performing?" Lilly asked, reading his expression.

"That was a long time ago. These days I have my hands full watching over Miley and Sir Toots-a-Lot," he joked.

Miley walked over to him. "Come on, Dad. We're practically adults. I mean if you want to go out and 'howl with the dogs,' there's nothing holding you back."

Miley's plea was punctuated by another armpit fart from Jackson.

"Sweetheart, that was ten years ago," Mr. Stewart said. "I bet my old manager doesn't even remember my name."

Just then the doorbell rang. "Robby Ray, open this door!" yelled a man's voice.

Miley pretended to be surprised. "Well, is that your old manager, Marty Klein?"

"I believe it is!" Jackson added innocently.

Lilly was in on the conspiracy, too. "What a weird coinkydink," she said.

Mr. Stewart eyed the three of them, trying to figure out which one was the worst actor. He gave up and decided it was a tie. "You guys are smooth," he said sarcastically, then opened the front door.

Marty Klein burst in like a salesman ready to talk someone into buying the Brooklyn Bridge. "Where's my Honkytonk Heartthrob?" he asked. "There he is! Look at you," he said, moving around Mr. Stewart and checking him out from every angle. "You look exactly the same. No, you look better! Give me a hug!"

"Madman Marty, the one-man party," Mr. Stewart said, when he was able to pull himself out of Marty's bear hug. "I've missed you, buddy."

"Stop it, you'll make me cry, and look, there's handsome young Jackson," Mr. Klein said, taking in the Stewart family. "And pretty little Miley, who I have not spoken to or had contact with in any way whatsoever, especially on the phone."

Mr. Stewart shook his head. Marty Klein was another bad actor.

"Okay, Marty," Miley said. "He knows I called you."

"Good, 'cause I'm a terrible liar." Mr. Klein suddenly noticed Lilly and his manager instincts kicked in. "Hi, sweetheart. Blondes are big this year. If ya got any talent, call me." He flipped Lilly a business card.

Miley tried to get him back on track. "So, Marty," she said pointedly. "Got anything interesting to tell my father?"

"Don't rush me, kid," Mr. Klein said. "I'm building to the big finish." He turned to Mr. Stewart. "So I called the Roadhouse in San Diego. You say the word and all next week, you, Robby Ray, are the special guest star."

Mr. Klein was clearly impressed with his own managing skills. "Ladies and gentlemen," he said, taking a bow, "Marty Klein."

But Robby Ray wasn't ready to say the word. This was all coming at him too fast. "Whoa, let's just slow down a minute."

"You walked away at the top because you wanted to be with your babies," Mr. Klein said. "Well, take a look. They're not babies anymore."

Miley squared her shoulders and used her most mature voice. "I believe Mr. Klein is correct, Father."

"Oh, come on, Dad," Jackson added.

"You know you want to be back onstage again. Here's your chance."

"Think about it, handsome," Mr. Klein urged. "You, the lights, the stage, the screaming crowd ..." He gestured to Miley, Jackson and Lilly.

"Rob-by, Rob-by," they chanted on cue. "Rob-by."

"Okay. Okay. Okay," Mr. Stewart said, trying to calm them all down. "I appreciate what you're all trying to do, but –"

"– you'll think about it. Fantastic!" Mr. Klein said, cutting him off before he could say no. "That's all I wanted to hear. And now I'm leaving before I hear anything else. Good-bye, good luck, ladies and gentlemen, Marty Klein." He took a quick bow and then ran out of the house.

Miley started to talk as fast as her father's old manager. "So, you've thought about it, you'll do it, you love me for thinking of it," she said. "Ladies and gentlemen, Miley Stewart."

Miley made a quick bow and grabbed Lilly's arm, ready to make a fast getaway. "C'mon, Lilly," she said, but she wasn't fast enough.

"Whoa, whoa, whoa, whoa, whoa," her father said, stopping her. "Slow down. Even if I was considering singing again, I'd get up on the stage and I wouldn't know what to say."

"I do," Jackson joked, pulling the string on the Robby Ray doll.

"Y'all ready to howl with the dog?" the doll asked.

Jackson, Miley and Lilly howled in unison. *"Ahooooooooooooooooooooooo!"*

All Mr. Stewart could do was shake his head and smile.

Chapter Three

That afternoon, Mr. Stewart sat on the sun deck overlooking the ocean, strummed his guitar and thought about the old days. He didn't notice Miley slip outside to listen to him sing.

"You are the meanest man I have ever met," Miley said.

Her father looked up, surprised. "Why?" he asked.

"To keep a talent so incredibly awesome

as this away from a world that needs you so desperately – it's just so selfish. I can't even look at you," Miley said, turning her back on him. But she couldn't resist. She snuck a peek to see if her plan was working.

"Okay, darlin', let's say I was thinking about singing again," Mr. Stewart said. "I can't take you guys with me and I sure can't leave you home alone for a week."

Jackson popped out of the living room with part two of their plan. "And you won't have to," he said. "I did a little research, made a few phone calls and I think I came up with the perfect solution." He squared his shoulders proudly. "May I present, direct from the International House of Nannies, the lovely and responsible Inga."

Upon hearing her name, a tall, beautiful, blond girl came out onto the deck. *"God dag, hur sta de till?"* she asked in Swedish.

Miley frowned. This wasn't the kind of nanny she and Jackson had talked about.

Mr. Stewart shook his head. "Nice try, Jackson. But there's no way I can leave this young lady here alone to nanny you."

But Jackson had that worked out, too. "You know, I thought you might say that. Which is why I hired *three* nannies." He stepped back and Inga's sisters Helga and Uma joined them on the deck.

Miley's eyes popped in amazement. So did Mr. Stewart's. Inga was one of a set of identical triplets.

"*God dag, hur sta de till?*" Helga and Uma said together.

Jackson put his arms around all three of them, totally pleased with himself. "Now I don't know about you, but I feel very, very, very nannied."

"Ladies, I appreciate you taking the time

to come over here, but this just ain't gonna work out," Mr. Stewart said. *"Tak sa-yalv for koo-moe."*

Now it was Jackson's turn to be amazed.

"Robby Ray was huge in Sweden," his father said, going back into the house.

"Robby Ray?" Inga asked.

"Honky-tonk Heartthrob!" Uma added.

"Ya, ya!" Helga said, recognizing Mr. Stewart.

Miley leaned in and glared at Jackson while the nannies chattered about Robby Ray in Swedish. "One thing," Miley said. "You only had one thing to get."

"Yeah, and I got three!" Jackson said in his own defence. "Forgive me for being an overachiever." He turned to the triplets. It was silly to lose the opportunity to spend time with three beautiful girls just because his father had said no. "So, ladies, who wants to boogie board with the son of the Honky-tonk Heartthrob?"

"Yeah, sure," Inga said in her Swedish accent.

"You betcha," Uma said.

"By golly. Ya, ya!" Helga added.

Jackson beamed. "Yeah, come on."

Miley frowned, watching them leave, and then followed her father into the house. She wasn't ready to give up yet. She knew her father wanted to perform again and she wasn't going to be the one who kept Robby Ray from howling with the dogs.

"C'mon, Daddy," she said. "I know you really want to do this."

"Mile, why are you pushing so hard?"

"Because of the way I feel when I'm onstage," Miley explained, thinking about the thrill that ran through her every time she stepped in front of an audience. And the even bigger thrill she felt at the end of a concert, when she knew she had given her fans the very best show she could. Her fans loved her for it and Miley loved them back. "I mean, don't you remember that feeling? Don't you want it again?"

"Well, of course I do. But –"

"But nothing," Miley said, cutting him off. She used his own words to convince him to change his mind. It was what he said to her and Jackson whenever they backed away from something new, or different, or hard. "But's just a word you use when you're afraid to try. That's something I learned from my daddy."

Mr. Stewart grinned. "Oh, so now you listen to me."

Miley nodded. "And you should, too," she said seriously.

"Okay, if you want to know the truth,"

Mr. Stewart admitted, "I did make some calls, but I just couldn't find anybody I'd trust to watch you kids."

"So, you're saying if you could find someone, you'd go?" Miley asked.

"Sure. It would have been fun, but it's just not on the cards."

Miley grinned. Now she had him – he had no choice but to say yes when he saw the ace she had hidden up her sleeve. "Well, shuffle them again, Daddy, and say hello to my backup plan." Miley opened the door with a flourish. Roxy stood just outside.

"Don't worry, hot stuff," Roxy said to him, striding into the room. "Roxy'll take care of everything. You just go get your mullet back."

The next morning, Mr. Stewart put a Post-it on the refrigerator with emergency phone numbers. "Okay, kids, I'll see you at the end of the week when you come down to the last show. Wish me luck!" he said.

"Knock 'em dead, Dad," Jackson said.

Miley gave her father a big hug. "You're going to do great."

Marty Klein opened the front door and stuck his head in to hurry Mr. Stewart along. "What a beautiful scene. A man and his children sharing a heartfelt goodbye. You know what it reminds me of?" he asked. "The fact that my car is running and petrol is three dollars a gallon. Let's move!"

Mr. Stewart laughed. So much for his heartfelt moment. "Ladies and gentlemen, Marty Klein." He kissed Miley on the forehead, patted Jackson's shoulder and headed for the door.

"Good luck, Dad!" Jackson said.

"Bye, Daddy. Love you!" Miley said, just

before he closed the door behind him. Then she turned to her brother. "Do you believe it? Dad's actually going to go out and perform again. I just wish I didn't have to wait a whole week to see him."

"Yeah, I'm in agony," Jackson said, pretending to feel the same way. "And now I'm over it. Oh, Cooper's throwing a party," he said, as he grabbed his car keys. "Don't wait up."

"Can you drop me off at Lilly's?" Miley asked.

"Slow your roll, children," Roxy said, coming into the room and blocking the door. "Your daddy left me in charge and that means until he gets home, you're not leaving my sight." Roxy locked them in. "I've got my eyes on you," she said, pointing to her own eyes and then at each one of them intently.

Jackson turned to Miley, confused. "What exactly does she mean by that?"

By the end of the day, Jackson had his answer. All three of them were crammed together on the sofa, which had been folded out into a bed. Roxy was in a sleeping bag on top of the covers between a very unhappy Jackson and an even more unhappy Miley.

Roxy's eyes were wide open, darting from Jackson to Miley and back to Jackson again. "Good night, kids," she said.

"Good night, Roxy," Miley and Jackson answered miserably.

Chapter Four

Hours later, Roxy snored away, with one arm holding Jackson in place and the other over Miley. Miley and Jackson stared at the ceiling. It was totally impossible to sleep with Roxy's buzz-saw snores roaring in their ears. They lifted their heads and signalled to each other with their eyes.

Slowly and carefully, they each lifted one of Roxy's arms and tried to ease out of bed without waking her. Their feet silently reached the floor and they were ready to stand up when Roxy – her eyes still closed – grabbed the back of their pyjamas and pulled them back onto the sofa bed.

"My eyes may be closed," she said. "But my brain is on red alert!" She didn't need to be able to see them to give Miley and Jackson the now-familiar "I've got my eyes on you" signal with each hand.

Seconds later, she was snoring again. Miley wondered if she should try another escape attempt when Roxy's arms suddenly shot up and sliced the air with a huge karate chop. "Hi-ya!" she yelled and then started to snore again.

The next morning, Roxy had finally stopped snoring and Miley and Jackson were trying to catch up on their sleep. But Roxy had other ideas. She looked down on her sleeping charges with a fond expression, then lifted a bugle and blasted them out of bed with "Reveille," as if they were Marines in basic training.

Jackson jumped up in a panic. "What is going on?" he yelled.

Miley was too tired to be startled. Roxy's snores had kept her up most of the night. "What time is it?" she asked, pulling the blanket up over her head.

"Six a.m.," Roxy announced. "It's time for our morning jog."

"Jog?" Jackson and Miley groaned at the same time.

"Now let's get those running shoes on and move, move, move!" Roxy ordered like a drill sergeant. "You're in Roxy's army now! Hurry up – last one down has to stretch out my hamstrings." Roxy raised her bugle and blasted the cavalry's "charge" call while she watched Miley and Jackson race up the stairs.

Later that afternoon, Roxy let Jackson out of her sight so he could head to the beach to work at Rico's. But he was having trouble keeping his eyes open. He wore dark sunglasses and leaned on the counter with his chin in both hands.

Lilly sat on a stool sipping a drink and chattering away. "I still can't believe your dad was up onstage last night. So how'd it go?" she asked. "Did he call?"

Jackson didn't answer. He just stood there, hiding behind his shades. It was like he couldn't hear Lilly at all.

"Jackson?" Lilly reached out to take off his sunglasses. He was sound asleep – standing up! Lilly grabbed a pair of girlie glasses off the display on the counter and slipped them behind Jackson's ears.

He still didn't budge.

"Boy, you're really out," she said, whipping out her camera phone.

She was just about to snap an embarrassing picture when Jackson pulled a Roxy. He didn't open his eyes. He didn't move. He just said, "Don't even think about it."

Miley was hanging out with Oliver a short distance away. She was as tired as Jackson was. "Roxy was like this all night," she told Oliver, demonstrating her incredibly loud snores, followed by a loud "Hi-ya!"

"Can't you just tell her to lighten up?" Oliver asked.

"Oh, sure," Miley whispered. "I tell her to lighten up, she gets upset, she leaves, Dad comes home early and once again, I've ruined his dream." Miley wasn't going to let that happen. Robby Ray had to have his music and his fans.

"Why are you whispering?" Oliver said.

"Because Roxy's everywhere." Miley pointed to her own eyes and then at Oliver's. "Because she's got her *eyyyyyes* on me."

Oliver realized his friend was seriously sleep-deprived, but this was going too far.

"Okay, now you're just paranoid," he said, looking around. "I don't see her anywhere."

"Oh, yeah?" Miley said, handing him a magazine. "Hit me with this magazine."

"What?" Oliver's forehead wrinkled in confusion. Miley wanted him to hit her?

"Just do it," Miley said. "Trust me, I'll be fine."

"Okay," Oliver said. He rolled up the magazine and raised his arm over his head, preparing to strike.

But before Oliver could even get his arm

all the way over his head, Roxy reached out and yanked him away from Miley.

"Ahhhhhh!" Oliver yelled.

Roxy flung him over the wall and watched him roll down the sand dune to the beach. Then she crouched, ready to take on anyone else who might harm Miley or Jackson. "I'm like a puma," Roxy hissed.

Jogging wasn't enough. Roxy spread out her physical activity all through the day. As soon as Jackson got off work, she had Miley and Jackson twisting and turning their bodies in incredibly hard yoga poses.

Jackson's head was stuck between his left knee and his right elbow. "I can't do this anymore," he whispered to Miley.

"It's only five more days," Miley whispered back. "Just do it for Dad."

"And shift," Roxy ordered.

Miley and Jackson tried to follow her

moves into another yoga posture. But her simple shifts seemed more like medieval tortures than yoga poses.

"Roxy, I didn't think that the Marines did yoga," Miley said with a groan.

"Oh, I didn't learn this in the Corps. I learned it when I was touring India with world-famous cellist Yo-Yo Ma," Roxy explained, twisting her left leg around her right arm. "He called me his Yo-Yo Mamma," she joked.

"This hurts," Jackson said, moaning.

"Oh, it's supposed to," Roxy answered. "Feel that negative energy leaving your body. Get out all that frustration and anger." Roxy twisted some more, but Miley's and Jackson's heads were stuck and they couldn't follow this latest move.

"Mmm. Now doesn't that feel good?" Roxy asked.

Good was definitely not what Miley was feeling. Actually, she was getting more frustrated and angry by the second, but she had to stick this out for her dad. That meant keeping Roxy happy. And dealing with the pain. "Uh-huh," she said.

"Yeah, in about an hour you'll be able to do this." Suddenly Roxy threw her legs over her head. Her feet were bent backwards over her shoulders and next to her ears. "Oh," she said, peering at her toenails. "I need a pedicure."

Jackson and Miley looked at each other, completely and totally horrified. There was no way they were ever going to get their bodies to do that. And they really, really, really didn't want to try.

They were saved by the doorbell.

"I'll get it," Jackson said, eager to escape.

Normally, Roxy would be the one to answer the door, but she let Jackson go ahead. "Yeah, you better, it's going to take me a little while to get out of this." She slowly started to untwist.

Miley watched Jackson head for the front door and then cringed when she heard two loud snapping, cracking sounds coming from Roxy's direction. But her bodyguard didn't seem to mind. In fact, judging by Roxy's loud sigh, she liked it. Still, there was no way Miley would ever get her body to do that.

Jackson's friends Angie, Stephanie and Jay were at the door.

"Hey, Jackson," Angie said. "We're going to the movies, thought you might want to –"

Jackson didn't have to hear the rest. He'd go just about anywhere with anyone to escape from Roxy and her torture yoga. "Yes! Yes! Yes! Yes!" he yelled.

But Roxy was faster than he was. Jackson was on his way out the door when Roxy grabbed the back of his shirt. "Where do you think you're going?" she asked.

"To the movies . . . with my friends . . . please?" Jackson pleaded.

"Okay, okay, I get it," Roxy said. "It's Saturday and you want to have a good time. I'm not going to stop you."

"Really?" Jackson asked, totally surprised. Maybe drill sergeant Roxy wasn't so bad after all.

Roxy nodded. "Really. Just let me get my purse," she said. "Miley, c'mon, we're going to the movies."

Jackson's jaw dropped. He was way too old to go to the movies with a babysitter. What would his friends think? "No, no, no, no, no," he said. "No way!"

"Uh, Roxy, I'm not really up for a movie," Miley said, trying to keep both her brother and her bodyguard happy. "And besides, I want to learn the, the foot thing you just did. You know, I always wanted to bite my own toenails."

"I promised your daddy I'd watch both of you and both of you is who I'm going to watch," Roxy said firmly.

"But —" Jackson said. He noticed his friends were exchanging shocked glances.

Roxy interrupted him. "Listen," she said to Jackson's friends, "I just need an aisle seat, okay? Roxy loves the big drink; but the big drink don't love Roxy."

Jackson watched his friends' expressions change from shock to horror. Going to the movies with a Marine Corps bodyguard wasn't exactly what they had in mind when they stopped by. They started to back out of the room.

"Okay, you know what . . . we just remembered we gotta . . ." Angie said, stammering.

"Because . . . ah, you know," Jay added, lamely.

"Bye!" They ran out of the house.

"But wait," Jackson called after them. It was too late; he heard Angie's car peeling out of the driveway. "I can't believe you just did that," he said to Roxy. "I cannot believe," he sputtered.

"You're angry, aren't you?" Roxy asked.

"Yeah!"

"That yoga didn't work for you, did it?"

"No!" Jackson yelled.

"That's because you need some acupuncture. I'll go and get my needles," Roxy said.

Jackson watched her go up the stairs.

That woman was not coming anywhere near him with needles. "That's it," he said to Miley. "Five days? I can't take five more minutes of this." He grabbed his jacket and his car keys.

"Jackson," Miley said, following him to the door, "where are you going?"

"San Diego! I want my daddy back!" He sang it to the tune of Robby Ray's biggest song.

"Jackson, you can't," Miley said.

Jackson pushed past her and out onto the deck.

"Ugh!" Miley followed her brother outside. She had to stop him! She had already ruined her father's singing career once. She wouldn't let that happen again. She *couldn't*.

"Jackson, you don't think I miss him, too? The way he sings to us in the morning when he's making pancakes, how happy he is when we come home from school." She smiled sadly, remembering another thing she missed. "No one's called me 'bud' in forty-eight hours."

"That's why I'm going to get him," Jackson said, running to his car.

"But Jackson, it's not about what *we* want," Miley called after him. "It's about what *he* wants."

A determined Jackson slammed his car door and started the engine.

Miley's shoulders slumped. She trudged back into the house to find Roxy running downstairs with her purse and her car keys. There were no acupuncture needles in sight.

"Turn it around, girl," Roxy said. "We've got to stop that boy."

"But Roxy, how did you –"

"I haven't just got my *eyes* on you," Roxy explained. "Let's move. It's a long drive."

Chapter Five

Jackson ran into the Roadhouse night-club. His father was onstage and the crowd was going wild.

Miley and Roxy ran in a few minutes behind Jackson. Roxy had insisted on stopping – twice – for food. The half-eaten cupcake in her hand had lost Miley three whole minutes. She had to stop Jackson before he asked their dad to come home.

Spotting Jackson, Miley ran over to

him. "Have you said anything to him yet?" she asked in a whisper.

"No, I just got here," Jackson said.

They listened for a minute. Miley got a thrill watching her father onstage. "He's really good."

"Are you kidding? He's great," Jackson said.

Not only was he a great singer, they both noticed he was having a great time. Robby Ray loved being onstage. Their father was happy – really, really happy.

Roxy leaned in and whispered. "Quiet! Robby Ray's got his groove on." Then she roared with the crowd. "Howl, doggy, howl!"

They settled in to watch Robby Ray's show, howling and cheering with the rest of his fans.

* * *

After the show, a lot of old and new fans swarmed Robby Ray's dressing room.

"Let's go, let the man rest," Mr. Klein said, shooing them out of the room. "Go! Go! Go!" he ordered, leaving with them. "Now!"

Miley and Jackson had to push their way through the departing crowd to get in to see their father.

"What are you doing here?" Mr. Stewart asked. "Is everything all right?"

"Well, ah, the truth is . . ." Jackson looked at Miley.

Miley gave her brother a pleading look. He couldn't blow this for their father. He just couldn't.

". . . we just couldn't wait to hear you play," Jackson finished. "You were great." He gave his dad a high five.

Miley smiled at Jackson, then gave her

father a big hug. "I'm so proud of you, Daddy."

Mr. Klein rushed back into the room. "Guess what I just heard? Toby Keith has a new opening act," he said in an excited rush. "And you know who it is? Don't guess, I'll tell you." He took a dramatic pause and then announced, "It's you!"

Mr. Stewart was visibly stunned. "Me?"

Mr. Klein nodded proudly. "Six beautiful weeks. One of which is in, yes, Hawaii." He took a bow. "Ladies and gentlemen, Marty Klein."

Miley eyed Roxy and swallowed. "Six weeks?"

"Wow," Jackson said. "That's —"

Miley jumped in before Jackson could finish. "Awesome," she said, blinking back her tears. "So incredibly . . . awesome . . . really." But she couldn't fight them. The tears overflowed and ran down her face. "They're going to love you in Hawaii," she cried, running out of the room before she could say what she really felt.

It wasn't awesome. It was awful. And that had nothing to do with Roxy and her six a.m. jogs and mid-afternoon torture-yoga classes. It was the idea of six weeks of not seeing his face when she got home from school and of not hearing anyone call her "bud." When her father was away, she missed him. She hated the idea of being separated from him for six whole weeks.

"Excuse me, Jackson," Mr. Stewart said, running after her. "Miley, wait up."

Roxy watched them go and then focussed on Jackson. "You kids sure must love your dad if you're willing to do six weeks of Roxy-time," she said.

"Are you kidding? If she hadn't started crying, I was going to," Jackson answered.

Mr. Stewart found Miley sitting on the edge of the stage in the empty nightclub.

"Hey, bud? You all right?"

"I'm sorry," Miley said, wiping away her tears.

"For what?" her father asked, sitting down next to her. "Crying? If you don't want me to go, just say so."

But Miley knew it wasn't that easy. If she just said so, her father would be giving up his dream for her – again. She couldn't ask him to do that. "Daddy, you gave up your whole life so I could have my dream. How can I stop you from having yours?"

"You kids *are* my dream. I didn't give up my career because I had to," he explained. "I gave it up because I wanted to."

He wanted to? Miley didn't understand. She couldn't imagine giving up Hannah Montana and her father had definitely been having a great time onstage. "But, I saw you up here tonight. You did so good. And you looked so happy," she said.

"I was. But I was a lot happier when I saw you kids coming through the door."

Miley was almost afraid to hope. "So, does that mean you don't want to do the tour anymore?"

"Six weeks away from you kids? I think I'd miss you too much," Mr. Stewart said.

"We'd miss you, too," Miley answered, smiling through her tears and giving her father a huge hug. She hoped her father would perform again one day, but right now, she was happy to have him at home. Then she realized there might be a way to keep her father at home and have Hawaii, too. "Well, maybe you could just do the Hawaii part and take us."

Her father was about to answer when Maddie from the Tipton Hotel rushed in. She and her mum had heard about Robby Ray's comeback and flown from Boston to San Diego to catch his show.

"Mum, quick, get in here," she called over her shoulder and dashed towards the stage. "Robby Ray is still here!"

They heard a howl from outside the club.

Roxy raced into the room and tackled Maddie to the floor. "Too close, candy girl!"

Later, Miley and her dad, wearing funky mullet wigs, took the stage in the empty nightclub and sang a duet of "I Want My Mullet Back." Jackson stood nearby, wearing a mullet wig of his own. With a nod from his father, he started to accompany the singers with armpit farts, while Roxy and Marty danced to the music.

Robby Ray might be retiring for a while, but the Stewart family was howling with the dogs.

Put your hands together for the next Hannah Montana book. . . .

Crush-tastic!

Adapted by Beth Beechwood

Based on the television series, "Hannah Montana", created by Michael Poryes and Rich Correll & Barry O'B

Based on the episode written by Sally Lapiduss

It was a regular day at Seaview Middle School – regular, except for the fact that Principal Fisher was retiring. All the students were busy creating farewell videos to pay tribute to him and Oliver was in charge of taping. He was wielding his camera all over school, driving everyone crazy. At the moment, his focus was on Lilly, who wasn't exactly eloquent in these types of situations.

"We're going to miss you, Principal Fisher," Lilly said. "I can't believe you're retiring. You don't look a day over eighty." Lilly thought this was the perfect thing to say.

Oliver leaned around his camera. "Lilly, he's only sixty-five!"

"Really?" Lilly said dramatically, her face dropping. "Is he sick?" She was *sure* he was older.

"He will be after he sees this," Oliver joked. . . .

"I want to do mine over again," Lilly pleaded to Oliver.

"We'll clean it up in editing," he said dismissively, suddenly noticing Miley. She was leaning against a wall, staring into space and chewing gum as if it were her job. She looked nervous. Oliver approached her. "Miley?" he asked. Nothing. He tried again. "Miley?"

But Miley ignored him. She was in another universe entirely. Oblivious to her friends, she took a deep breath and walked right past them . . . and right towards Jake. Jake, the star of a hit TV show, was a teen heartthrob. But his fame wasn't a secret the way Miley's was. All the girls loved him and fawned all over him. Miley did, too, but in her mind only. To his face, she tried to be the cool, collected girl who treated him like a regular guy. After all, she kind of understood how it could be – that's why she kept her "other" life a secret.